Dear Parents and Educators,

Welcome to Penguin Young Readers! As parents and educators, you know that each child develops at his or her own pace—in terms of speech, critical thinking, and, of course, reading. Penguin Young Readers recognizes this fact. As a result, each Penguin Young Readers book is assigned a traditional easy-to-read level (1–4) as well as a Guided Reading Level (A–P). Both of these systems will help you choose the right book for your child. Please refer to the back of each book for specific leveling information. Penguin Young Readers features esteemed authors and illustrators, stories about favorite characters, fascinating nonfiction, and more!

Cork & Fuzz: The Babysitters

LEVEL 3

GUIDED READING LEVEL **J**

This book is perfect for a **Transitional Reader** who:
- can read multisyllable and compound words;
- can read words with prefixes and suffixes;
- is able to identify story elements (beginning, middle, end, plot, setting, characters, problem, solution); and
- can understand different points of view.

Here are some **activities** you can do during and after reading this book:
- Creative Writing: In this story, Fuzz tries many different ways to make the baby porcupine laugh. For example, he sings a silly song. Pretend you are also trying to make the baby porcupine laugh. Write a paragraph describing what funny things you might do.
- Setting: The setting of a story is where it takes place. Discuss the setting of this story. Use some evidence from the text to describe the setting. How does the setting affect what happens in the story? For instance, why it is important that Cork, Fuzz, and the baby porcupine are near a tree?

Remember, sharing the love of reading with a child is the best gift you can give!

—Bonnie Bader, EdM
　　Penguin Young Readers program

*Penguin Young Readers are leveled by independent reviewers applying the standards developed by Irene Fountas and Gay Su Pinnell in *Matching Books to Readers: Using Leveled Books in Guided Reading*, Heinemann, 1999.

For Stacy DeKeyser, Kelly DiPucchio,
Marsha Hayles, Shirley Neitzel, and Lisa Wheeler—
in appreciation and friendship—DC

To Kristen, who knew us when,
and her daughter Taylor—LM

PENGUIN YOUNG READERS
Published by the Penguin Group
Penguin Group (USA) LLC, 375 Hudson Street, New York, New York 10014, USA

USA | Canada | UK | Ireland | Australia | New Zealand | India | South Africa | China

penguin.com
A Penguin Random House Company

The Library of Congress has cataloged the Viking edition under the following Control Number:
2009030386

ISBN 978-0-448-48050-3   10 9 8 7 6 5 4 3 2 1

PENGUIN YOUNG READERS

LEVEL 3

TRANSITIONAL READER

CORK & FUZZ
The Babysitters

by Dori Chaconas
illustrated by Lisa McCue

Penguin Young Readers
An Imprint of Penguin Group (USA) LLC

4

Chapter One

Cork was a short muskrat.

He liked to help.

He liked to help baby birds.

He liked to help keep the pond clean.

Fuzz was a tall possum.

He liked to help, too.

He liked to help himself to worms for breakfast.

He liked to help himself to trash-bin scraps for supper.

Two best friends.

One was helpful.

The other one was Fuzz.

One day Cork walked

to Fuzz's house.

He walked slowly.

He walked slowly because he was

holding a baby porcupine by the paw.

Fuzz was in his yard.

He was pulling leaves off a long vine.

"What are you doing?" Cork asked.

"I am busy," Fuzz said.

"Where did you find the pokie-pie?"

"I did not find him," Cork said.

"His mother gave him to me."

"To keep?" Fuzz asked.

"Not to keep," Cork said.

"I am helping.

I am babysitting."

Fuzz looked at the porcupine.

"I would not want to babysit on him,"
Fuzz said.

"I would get poked with a pokie."

"No, no, no," Cork said.

"Babysit does not mean you sit on
the baby.

It means you watch him."

"Erk!" said the baby porcupine.

He picked up a stone.

He put it in his mouth.

"Watch him eat stones?" Fuzz asked.

Cork took the stone

out of the baby's mouth.

"Watch him so he does not get hurt,"
Cork said.

"Will you help me babysit?"

"Not today," Fuzz said.

"I am busy making a bear trap."

Chapter Two

"What will you do with the bear when you trap it?" Cork asked.

"First I will trap the bear," Fuzz said. "Then I will think about what to do with it."

Fuzz made a loop with the vine.

He laid the loop on the ground.

"Erk!" said the baby porcupine.

He put a flower in his mouth.

Cork took the flower out of the

baby's mouth.

"Help me, Fuzz!" he said.

"I am busy," Fuzz said.

Fuzz put a large rock on the vine
next to the loop.

"Erk!" said the porcupine.

He put a pinecone in his mouth.

Cork took the pinecone out of the
baby's mouth.

"Please, Fuzz!" Cork said.

"I really need your help!"

"I am very, very busy," Fuzz said.

Fuzz climbed a tree.

He crawled to the end of a branch.

Fuzz tied the loose end of the vine to the tip of the branch.

"Erk!" said the porcupine.

He put some tree bark in his mouth.

Cork took the bark away.

"Please, please, please, Fuzz!" he said.

"If you help me babysit, I will give you my best green stone."

"Okay," said Fuzz.

He held out his paw for the stone.

"I was done anyway."

"Ack! Ack! Ack!"

The baby porcupine started to cry.

"He is chewing a bitter berry," Fuzz said.

"Please do not cry!" Cork said.

He took the bitter berry

out of the baby's mouth.

Then he wiped the porcupine's

tongue with his paw.

"ACK! ACK! ACK!" The porcupine

cried louder.

"Now he has got muskrat fur

on his tongue," Fuzz said.

"Help me, Fuzz," Cork said.

"Help me make him stop crying!"

Chapter Three

"Okay," said Fuzz.

"I will help.

I will stand on my head."

"How will that help?" Cork asked.

"It will help because I do not know

18

how to stand on my head," Fuzz said.

"I will fall over.

The pokie-pie will stop crying and

he will laugh."

Fuzz stood on his head.

He fell over.

The baby did not stop crying.

"That did not help," Cork said.

"I will sing him a song," Fuzz said.

"Do you know a song?" Cork asked.

"I will make one up," Fuzz said.

"Hey pokie-pokies.

The cat told some jokies.

The cow jumped in the lagoon."

"That does not make any sense,"
Cork said.

The baby cried even louder.

"I will do a step-kick
dance for him," Fuzz said.
"I will step with one foot.
I will kick with the other
foot."

Fuzz stepped on the grass.

He kicked a weed.

He stepped on the path.

He kicked a daisy.

Then he stepped in the vine loop.

He kicked the large stone.

The stone rolled.

The vine loop grabbed Fuzz's foot.

WHOOSH!

Fuzz hung upside down in the tree.

"You caught yourself in the bear

trap!" Cork said.

The baby porcupine stopped crying.

He clapped his paws.

He waved at Fuzz.

Then he laughed.

"Help me, Cork!" Fuzz yelled.

"Climb up the tree.

Untie the vine!"

"Muskrats cannot climb trees!"

Cork said.

"And I have to watch the pokie-pie."

Cork looked down at the porcupine.

"Oh no!" Cork said.

Chapter Four

Cork could not see the baby
anywhere.

"Help me!" Fuzz yelled.

"I want to help you," Cork called.

"But I have to find the baby!
Can you see him from up there?"

"Yes," Fuzz said.

"I can see the pokie-pie."

"Is he in the bushes?" Cork asked.

"No," Fuzz said.

"Is he in the tall grass?" Cork asked.

"No," Fuzz said.

Cork stamped his foot.

"Just tell me where he is!"
Cork yelled.

"He is right up here," Fuzz said.

Cork looked up.

The baby porcupine was crawling out on the tree branch.

"Pokie-pie!" Cork yelled.

"Come down here!"

The porcupine crawled to the end of the branch.

He grabbed the vine.

He chewed and chewed and chewed.

He chewed right through the vine.

"YEOW!" Fuzz fell into the bitter-berry bush.

"I am taking the pokie-pie back to his mother," Cork said.

"I am not a good babysitter."

"You are a good babysitter," Fuzz said.

"You even taught the pokie-pie to be a good helper. He helped me get out of the trap."

Cork smiled.

"Then I do not feel so bad," he said.

"Now I am the only one who feels bad," Fuzz said.

"Why do you feel bad?" Cork asked.

Fuzz answered, "Because I did not catch a bear."

Cork patted Fuzz on the back.

"We can sing to make you feel better." And so they did.

Two best friends, singing and swinging the porcupine home.